THE STORY OF THE
DANCING
FROG

written and illustrated by Quentin Blake

DRAGONFLY BOOKS · ALFRED A. KNOPF
New York

DR. M. JERRY WEISS, Distinguished Service Professor of Communications at Jersey City State College, is the educational consultant for Dragonfly Books. A past chair of the International Reading Association President's Advisory Committee on Intellectual Freedom, he travels frequently to give workshops on the use of trade books in schools.

A DRAGONFLY BOOK PUBLISHED BY ALFRED A. KNOPF, INC.
Copyright © 1984 by Quentin Blake
All rights reserved under International and Pan-American Copyright Conventions. Published in the United States by Alfred A. Knopf, Inc., New York. Distributed by Random House, Inc., New York. Originally published in Great Britain by Jonathan Cape Ltd., London, in 1984. Published in hardcover as a Borzoi Book by Alfred A. Knopf, Inc., in 1985.

Library of Congress Cataloging-in-Publication Data
Blake, Quentin.   The story of the dancing frog.
Summary: Relates the adventures of Great Aunt Gertrude and her dancing frog as they travel the world and gain fame and fortune.
1. Children's stories, English   [1. Frogs—Fiction]   I. Title.
PZ7.B56St   1984   [E]   84-12222
ISBN 0-394-87033-6 (trade)   ISBN 0-394-97033-0 (lib. bdg.)
ISBN 0-394-84506-4 (pbk.)

First Dragonfly edition: February 1990
Manufactured in the United States of America
1 2 3 4 5 6 7 8 9 10

"Tell me another story about our family," said Jo.

"I'm really too tired, lovey."

"If I make the cocoa and the sandwiches?"

"Well–all right then. What have I told you? Uncle Geoffrey and the iceberg. And Sarah and her lions. Do you know about Great-aunt Gertrude Godkin and the dancing frog?"

"No. Can I have that, please?"

"You get the cocoa and I'll see how much I can remember.

"When Gertrude was a young woman she married an officer in the navy. He was very handsome, with a black beard and a smart uniform.

"The trouble with being married to a sailor is that he has to go with his ship, so that a lot of time you can't be with the person you want most to be with. Anyway, they were happy when they were together, and they had a house by the sea and Gertrude would watch for his ship returning, and when he came home he brought her presents from abroad."

"What sort of presents?"

"Little brass tables with folding legs, wooden camels, ornamental daggers.

"One day the ship didn't come back. Gertrude waited and waited. Then there was a letter from the navy to say that the ship had sunk and Gertrude's sailor was drowned. You can imagine how awful it must have been to get a letter like that."

"Yes."

"She went out of the house and started walking along by the river. There can't have seemed anything in life worth living for, and she was on the point of throwing herself in, so that she could be drowned too, like her husband, and finished.

"But she noticed something which stopped her. On one of the lily pads in the river was a frog. It was dancing.

"Gertrude stood and watched it as it danced and then— I don't think she quite knew why—she walked into the water and picked up the frog and carried it home.

"That night Gertrude kept the frog in a bucket in the kitchen, and the next day she dug a pond for it in the garden. For the rest of the day Gertrude stayed by the pond, watching the frog swim around. From time to time it would do a little dance on the grass.

"That evening, after she had had something to eat, Gertrude put a record on the wind-up gramophone she had been given as a wedding present. Then she went out into the garden and picked up the frog in her hands and brought him in and put him on the kitchen table. And the frog slowly started to do a new kind of dance—a dance to the music.

"And then we don't know quite how it happened—but the frog went on the stage. Perhaps Gertrude knew someone at the local theater—and a dancing frog *is* a rather unusual thing. And no doubt Gertrude didn't have much money after her husband disappeared and she was glad of anything they could earn. Anyway, for the first time the frog's name appeared on a theater poster. Right at the bottom: GEORGE, THE DANCING FROG."

"Was that his name then?"

"I don't know. Maybe it was just his stage name. After that they traveled around the country, wherever they could get work. It must have been a hard life for Gertrude— carrying the luggage, staying in cheap lodgings, arguing with landladies who didn't want a frog in their rooms.

"But they made lots of friends. At one theater George took part in the magician's act. He dived through a hoop and then the magician made him disappear.

"At another theater he jumped out of a hat when the comedian pretended to be drunk."

"What Daddy used to call plastered."

"Yes, that's right, lovey. George learned lots of new dances—the soft-shoe, the cakewalk, the polka.

"And then one day Gertrude was told something that
changed their lives: there was a job at a big theater in the
city. A talking dog had been taken ill with a sore throat
and they were desperate for a replacement. George got the
job. He did all his dances and suddenly everybody wanted
to see him.

"It was a different life. People sent flowers to George's dressing room and waited to see him at the stage door. Newspaper reporters interviewed Gertrude about him. Society hostesses wanted him at their parties.

"George was taken to expensive restaurants. A famous chef even invented a dish especially for him, of worms in butter sauce."

"Ugh. Imagine cooking worms."

"They weren't cooked. Frogs won't eat anything that's dead. They were alive.

"At least they weren't poor any longer—but there was even more work for Gertrude. Arranging for the money they were to be paid; arranging for trains; arranging for luggage. But it must have been exciting, traveling around the world ...strange cities, warm nights under starry skies.

"In Paris, George danced with a woman in the Follies,
and the audience went wild with excitement.

"He also did a wonderful dance with another woman who waved shawls. He danced with Spanish dancers and you could hear his croaking above the sound of the castanets.

"In Russia he danced in a special version of *Swan Lake*. He jumped higher than any of the ballet dancers.

"It was in Monte Carlo that Gertrude had her offer. An English lord asked her to marry him.

" 'This is no life for a woman,' he said. 'I have a house in the country and another in London, and everything shall be provided for you. Leave all this and live with me as Lady Belvedere.' It must have been a great temptation.

"Who was to know how long George would go on being successful? But they were just getting ready for their tour of the U.S.A., and somehow she knew she couldn't really give up. So Lord Belvedere had to be content with no for an answer.

"The dreadful business of the fire happened in New York. George was rehearsing a new musical. The night the show opened, the hotel where they were staying caught fire.

"Gertrude was out in the street buying the evening papers. She saw smoke pouring out of the hotel doors and windows. How could she possibly get back to George, who was in their room on the thirteenth floor? Then suddenly she saw him on the ledge by the open window.

"By then the fire engines had arrived. Gertrude snatched a bucket of water from a fireman and called out at the top of her voice.

"It must have been the most extraordinary thing he ever did, on the stage or off it. A 120-foot jump into a bucket of water with perfect precision.

"George went on that night and was more brilliant
than ever. At the end of the show the audience stood and
applauded for twenty minutes.

"And it went on like that. Nobody much remembers them nowadays, but they really were a great success."

"Was Gertrude ever sorry that she didn't marry Lord Belvedere?"

"I don't think she ever told anybody she was."

"She preferred the frog."

"Well, I suppose you could say they looked after each other over the years."

"And what happened to them in the end?"

"The last time anybody in the family saw them was before the war. They had a little house in the South of France, with a water tank for George.

"Gertrude used to grow hollyhocks and sort out their
newspaper cuttings. In the warm weather she would give
George a shower with the watering can."

"And are they dead now?"

"Well, that was a long time ago, so I suppose they must be."

Jo collected the cocoa mugs and the plates.

"Was that a true story?"

"More or less."

"But frogs don't really dance, do they?"

"Not normally, no."

"And no one could really catch a frog and put it on the stage."

"You can do all kinds of things if you need to enough."